R0084791359

02/2017

W9-AXR-583

Margaret Hillert's
City Fun

A Beginning-to-Read Book

Illustrated by Karen Lewis

DEAR CAREGIVER,

The books in this Beginning-to-Read collection may look somewhat familiar in that the original versions could have been a part of your own early reading experiences. These carefully written texts feature common sight words to provide your child multiple exposures to the words appearing most frequently in written text. These new versions have been updated and the engaging illustrations are highly appealing to a contemporary audience of young readers.

Begin by reading the story to your child, followed by letting him or her read familiar words and soon your child will be able to read the story independently. At each step of the way, be sure to praise your reader's efforts to build his or her confidence as an independent reader. Discuss the pictures and encourage your child to make connections between the story and his or her own life. At the end of the story, you will find reading activities and a word list that will help your child practice and strengthen beginning reading skills. These activities, along with the comprehension questions are aligned to current standards, so reading efforts at home will directly support the instructional goals in the classroom.

Above all, the most important part of the reading experience is to have fun and enjoy it!

Shannon Cannon

Shannon Cannon,
Literacy Consultant

Norwood House Press • www.norwoodhousepress.com
Beginning-to-Read™ is a registered trademark of Norwood House Press.
Illustration and cover design copyright ©2017 by Norwood House Press. All Rights Reserved.

Authorized adapted reprint from the U.S. English language edition, entitled City Fun by Margaret Hillert. Copyright © 2017 Margaret Hillert. Reprinted with permission. All rights reserved. Pearson and City Fun are trademarks, in the US and/or other countries, of Pearson Education, Inc. or its affiliates. This publication is protected by copyright, and prior permission to re-use in any way in any format is required by both Norwood House Press and Pearson Education. This book is authorized in the United States for use in schools and public libraries.

Designer: Lindaanne Donohoe
Editorial Production: Lisa Walsh

LIBRARY OF CONGRESS CATALOGING-IN-PUBLICATION DATA
Names: Hillert, Margaret, author. I Lewis, K. E., illustrator.
Title: City fun / by Margaret Hillert ; illustrated by KE Lewis.
Description: Chicago, IL : Norwood House Press, [2016] I Series: A
   Beginning-to-Read book I Originally published in 1981 by Follett
   Publishing Company. I Summary: "Two friends explore a city by watching
   construction, riding the subway, going to a park, seeing a parade and
   visiting the library"-- Provided by publisher.
Identifiers: LCCN 2016001847 (print) I LCCN 2016022101 (ebook) I ISBN
   9781599538136 (library edition : alk. paper) I ISBN 9781603579841 (eBook)
Subjects: I CYAC: City and town life--Fiction.
Classification: LCC PZ7.H558 Cj 2016 (print) I LCC PZ7.H558 (ebook) I DDC
   [E]--dc23
LC record available at https://lccn.loc.gov/2016001847

288N—072016
Manufactured in the United States of America in North Mankato, Minnesota.

I like it here.
I like what I see.
I like what I do.
I have fun.

See what we can play.
We have to jump.
Jump, jump, jump.

And we can do this.
Look at us go.
We have to work at this.

Here is something
to look at.
See it go up.
Up, up, up.

And look at this.
It will come down.
Down, down, down.

Away, away, away.
We will ride away.
What a good ride.

I see something.
Red ones, yellow ones,
blue ones.
I will get one later.

I want this, too.
I like this.
It is good.

Now see what we can do.
It is fun to do this.
Look out. Look out.

Oh, look at that.
Here it comes.
What fun. What fun.

Look at this.
See what I can do.
I like it.
I like it.

It is fun up here.
Way, way up here.
And I like to look down.

I like to see the boats.
Big boats.
Little boats.
Go, boats, go.

Oh, what fun!
Up and down.
Up and down.

We can go up
and down, too.
We can jump, jump, jump.
1 and 2 and 3 and 4 …

Here is a man.
What will he do?
What can he do for us?

Oh, oh, oh.
Look at this.
Come in. Come in.
It is good in here.

And here comes something.
We like this.
We will get something
good to eat.

Come here. Come here.
Guess what we can do
in here.
Guess. Guess.

We can get something.
You will like it.
You can take it with you.

I like it out here.
It is fun to sit here.
It is fun to do
what we do.

Foundational Skills

In addition to reading the numerous high-frequency words in the text, this book also supports the development of foundational skills.

Phonological Awareness: The /w/ sound

Sound Substitution: Say these words: **want, way, we, what, will, with,** and **work**. Ask your child to repeat the beginning sound in each word after you say it. Say the words on the left to your child. Ask your child to repeat the word, changing the first sound to /**w**/:

tin = win	fire = wire	bent = went	jeep = weep
sag = wag	paste = waste	cave = wave	mild = wild
pick = wick	bill = will	pink = wink	make = wake
talk = walk	pet = wet	vest = west	me = we

Phonics: The letter Ww

1. Demonstrate how to form the letters **W** and **w** for your child.
2. Have your child practice writing **W** and **w** at least three times each.
3. Ask your child to point to the words in the book that begin with the letter **w**.
4. Write down the following words with the spaces representing missing letters. Ask your child to fill in the spaces by writing a **w**. Ask your child to read each word aloud.

__eb	__ind	__ait	__eak	ho__	ne__
blo__	se__	to__n	to__er	t__ig	to__el

Fluency: Choral Reading

1. Reread the story with your child at least two more times while your child tracks the print by running a finger under the words as they are read. Ask your child to read the words he or she knows with you.
2. Reread the story aloud together. Be careful to read at a rate that your child can keep up with.
3. Repeat choral reading and allow your child to be the lead reader and ask him or her to change from a whisper to a loud voice while you follow along and change your voice.

Language

The concepts, illustrations, and text help children develop language both explicitly and implicitly.

Vocabulary: Verb Tense

1. On a blank sheet of paper, make three columns by drawing two lines. Write the following story words at the top of each column: **do**, **does**, **did**. Ask your child to read the words aloud.

2. Write each of the following story words in the first column under the word do: **jump**, **see**, **play**, **go**, **ride**, **eat**, **look**, **come**. For each word, ask your child to provide the other verb forms for each column. You may want to offer prompts such as: **I like to jump high**. **My dog jumps high in the air**. **Yesterday, I jumped over a puddle**.

3. Write each of the following verbs on separate index cards: jump/jumps/jumped, see/sees/saw, play/plays/played, go/goes/went, ride/rides/rode, eat/eats/ate, look/looks/looked, come/comes/came.

   Mix up the index cards and ask your child to group them in verb families. Ask your child to place the verbs in each family according to tense (present, present + s, past) and read them aloud in order.

Reading Literature and Informational Text

To support comprehension, ask your child the following questions. The answers either come directly from the text or require inferences and discussion.

Key Ideas and Detail

- Ask your child to retell the sequence of events in the story.
- What things did the girls in the story buy?

Craft and Structure

- Is this a book that tells a story or one that gives information? How do you know?
- Do you think the girls in the story are friends? Why or why not?

Integration of Knowledge and Ideas

- Who was the character in the story riding on the horse?
- What are some things to do in your city or a city nearby?

City Fun uses the 59 words listed below.

This list can be used to practice reading the words that appear in the text. You may wish to write the words on index cards and use them to help your child build automatic word recognition. Regular practice with these words will enhance your child's fluency in reading connected text.

a	for	jump	play	up
and	fun			us
at		later	red	
away	get	like	ride	want
	go	little		way
big	good	look	see	we
blue	guess		sit	what
boats		man	something	will
	have	me		with
can	he		take	work
come(s)	here	now	that	
			the	
do	I	oh	this	yellow
down	in	one(s)	to	you
	is	out	too	
eat	it			

ABOUT THE AUTHOR Margaret Hillert has helped millions of children all over the world learn to read independently. She was a first grade teacher for 34 years and during that time started writing books that her students could both gain confidence in reading and enjoy. She wrote well over 100 books for children just learning to read. As a child, she enjoyed writing poetry and continued her poetic writings as an adult for both children and adults.

Photograph by Glenna Washburn

ABOUT THE ILLUSTRATOR Karen Lewis started drawing when she was three, and never stopped! She thinks being an artist is the best job ever, and a terrific excuse to learn all about anything that interests her. She loves illustrating books and making animation— especially for kids—and is a cartoonist for a children's history magazine. Karen lives in Seattle with her husband, young son, three cats and nine chickens. www.karenlewis.com